The Jacobite Officer

The Jacobite Officer

Matthew John Donnachie

For my mum Anna and Edith Garrow
who always believed in me

Published in 2018 by Fairy Pool Productions
© Matthew John Donnachie 2018

Publishing Services provided by Lumphanan Press
www.lumphananpress.co.uk

Printed & bound by ImprintDigital.com, UK

ISBN: 978-1-9164782-1-3

Contents

Prologue *9*

Glenfinnan *11*

The Faerie Pools *15*

The Crossing (Ferry for the Dead) *22*

Gask (The Clach an Airm) *23*

Clava Cairns *26*

Rait Castle (Feast of the Bull) *29*

Gille Dubh *31*

Eilean Donan *34*

Struan *35*

Cú Chulainn's Dream *39*

Prestonpans *41*

Oisín *45*

Barevan and Cù Sìth *48*

Culloden *54*

Culloden House *57*

The Officer Stone *58*

Elizabeth Campbell *60*

The Brahn Seer *61*

Dun Sgathaich *66*

Glen Dessary *74*

Tech Duinn (The House of Donn) *78*

Author Background *83*

Acknowledgements *87*

"Deep into that darkness peering, long I stood there, wondering, fearing, doubting, dreaming dreams no mortal ever dared to dream before."

– *Edgar Allan Poe, 1809–1849*

Prologue

SCOTLAND, A LAND FULL OF MYSTERY, A LAND STEEPED in legends as old as time itself.

As the mist settles on the hills and a veil of darkness descends upon the glens, tales of beasts, fairies and ghosts remain. Oral tradition in the Highlands is still strong; the stories of old live with us and are part of who we are as a people. Many of these legends remain unexplained.

I too have become something not easily explained.

To the spirit world, you mortals are as shadows. I am Donnachaidh Mhor, a Jacobite Officer destined to fight and die for my Prince. Or at least I was until that fateful day, the day I was forever to live another man's curse.

Now I watch as children dare one another to whisper my name by candlelight. I have become a grandfather's tale, passed down through generations. I stand in the forgotten glen, neither alive nor dead, haunted by the ghosts of the past, hunted by a beast of my present.

I am the Jacobite Officer who walks with shadows in the Otherworld, cursed to wander through time. I am but a reflection in a stream, the cold breath of a morning. There was a gateway to another world, and I was taken through the darkness by a mythical creature, never to return to my mortal realm. Before the mists come back to claim me once more I shall tell you of my journey.

Glenfinnan

I AM THE SON OF THE POET CHIEF, STRUAN OF ROBERTSON.
I was brought up as a Jacobite, loyal to the House of Stewart. I have no love for the Hanoverian usurpers and murderers in the south. My father fought at Killiecrankie in 1689 and was imprisoned in 1715 after the Battle of Sheriffmuir, during which time I was forced to find refuge with Clan Cameron in Arisaig in Moidart.

In the late summer of 1745 the news came that Charles Edward had landed on Eriskay to reclaim the throne for the House of Stewart. Rumours spread through the Highlands that a rising had begun… I vowed that I would take my place with my father, Struan of Robertson and rise up with the men of Atholl.

But not all were so true to the cause.

The powerful Chiefs of Skye, the Macleods and the Macdonalds, said they would not rise for the Prince and followed their word. Damn them for their cowardice and treachery!

I rose before dawn at A'Chuil in Glen Dessary on 17th August 1745. I pulled my good sword and pistol from the thatch and saddled my horse. Before I left I went back into the house and kissed my bonnie wife Jenny Cameron on the cheek as she slept. She is my love and everything I hold dear.

"Watch over the boys," I whispered, "I'll be back as soon as I can."

I had a sick feeling of dread in my stomach leaving them. But I had to go. God willing, I would return to A'Chuil.

I rode for a day on the Fort William road, towards the Prince's Jacobite army at Glenfinnan. I planned to join the

(11)

The Jacobite Officer

men of Clan Cameron, my wife's clan, until the Atholl men arrived, for Lochiel gave me shelter when I was hunted and I lived under his protection. He is a true Highland Chief and a good man. If only there were more like him. I would represent my father Struan till the men of Atholl rose.

I rode on through the mists of the day.

As I passed through a darkened pass of trees my horse faltered; I could feel her body tremble nervously. There was a crunch of feet and shadows moved in the trees, plaided figures, a glint of steel. Muskets were cocked. A voice shouted out, "State your business in Cameron country and make no move, or by God I will put a hole through your skull!"

"I am Donnachaidh Mhor, son of Struan of Robertson, and I live in Cameron country, under the protection of Lochiel himself."

A figure moved out of the shadows towards me, "I am Lochiel's son and I know who you are, Donnachaidh Mhor. Why does a Chief's son such as you risk his life by riding alone this trail?" he said, circling menacingly around my horse.

"I have heard that the Stewart Prince has landed in Eriskay. It is my duty to rise for him, even if I am to rise alone," said I.

In an instant I spun my horse, knocking him to the ground while pulling my pistol. As he staggered to his feet I pointed my pistol at his head, "I do believe I couldn't miss your big heid from here John Cameron." The plaided shadows laughed as I reholstered my pistol and John Cameron rose to his feet.

"It shows that you are married to a Cameron, Donnachaidh. She has kept your wits keen."

Another face then appeared from the darkness, one that I recognised as Lochiel himself, "Ah 'tis yourself young Struan. I trust cousin Jenny is looking after you and the boys?"

"Indeed she is, and she would have risen too in a moment but her place is with them. I left before she woke lest I would face her wrath."

(12)

"Aye, the wrath of a woman is always best avoided," laughed Lochiel, "especially Jenny Cameron's. We shall march together to meet the Prince at the head of Loch Shiel at Glenfinnan. Ride with me young Struan. Lochiel and the sons of Chiefs shall meet the Prince together."

We rode all day, men constantly joining us till the early evening when we came to the Sgùrr an Utha. There was nearly a thousand of us all told. The pipes were playing and the Cameron standards were raised above us.

I could see another gathering of men on the flat ground beyond the shore. They cheered as we approached, 'twas then I saw Charles Edward Stewart for the first time. A tall, fair, reddish-haired man, a man who would be king, "Our rightful king has returned to us!" I cheered. Amongst this sea of tartan warriors who would fight and die for their king, all things seemed possible. There was a smell of brandy in the air as we cheered and threw our bonnets skywards.

I watched as the royal standard fluttered in the breeze while men wept and swore allegiance to their young Prince. Later that evening, Lochiel introduced me to Charles Edward himself, "This is Donnachaidh Mhor, your Highness, son of the great Struan of Robertson."

"I know your family well," the Prince said, "and I recognise how much your clan have dedicated to my family's cause. My father asked for your father by name and said he was his oldest and dearest friend in Scotland."

In tears I fell to my knees, overwhelmed by the presence of one so close to the divine, "Your Highness, I am my father's son, yours to command. I will die to protect you."

The Prince, now also with tears in his eyes, pulled me to my feet and embraced me, "Call me Carlo, that's what my father calls me," he whispered.

At a council meeting that evening the Prince recognised my clan's loyalty to his cause and I was proud to be commissioned as an officer in his army. I was given the great honour of being chosen to deliver a letter in the Prince's own hand for MacDonald of Sleat.

"As you are the Poet Chief's son and a man of Atholl with no local quarrel, he will surely listen to you," said Lochiel.

The Prince rose from the table and handed me the letter, "Give this to Sleat, Donnachaidh, he surely cannot deny my father's call to rise."

My time of great service had come, to deliver this letter in the name of King James III and VIII of Scotland. Surely the Macdonalds would rise.

But the letter was destined never to reach him.

The Faerie Pools

I CROSSED THE MINCH AND RODE NORTH THROUGH Skye. The sky was heavy and dark, and it seemed like the damned rain would never stop. Cold and soaked to the skin though I was, as the King's messenger it was my duty to continue.

As I rode past the faerie pools I could hear a woman's voice on the wind, then the screams of a horse. My own steed reared up in response, throwing me to the ground, knocking the very breath from me. My mount was gone. Winded, I staggered to my feet.

The screams got louder and louder as I was drawn to them. Why, I know not.

In the distance I could see dancing lights of many colours, and a fine mist hung in the air. A woman's faint voice struggled through, "Help me... help me..."

Drawing closer, I saw that the noise came from no mere horse. It was the mythical creature known as the Kelpie, the water horse. Her bridle had become tangled in a snare of reeds. Kelpies were known to drown mortals, but I was not afraid. Words of the spirit filled my head, "Set me free, set me free Donnachaidh Mhor, and I shall reward you with riches beyond imagination."

I waded through the misty water towards the beast and pulled my dirk. The Kelpie screamed and thrashed as I came closer but I meant her no harm. I could hardly breath. The cold black water was taking my very breath.

She was then before me, a huge horse bathed in blue light. I reach down into the waters and hacked the reeds from her

(15)

bridle. Freed, her great wings beat as she arose from the water and began to change before my eyes into a beautiful young woman with flowing golden hair in tresses.

I reached out to touch her face, that porcelain skin as white as snow, and she spoke, "Son of man, you shall be rewarded for your kindness, for deep within this pool lies knowledge. Its divine secrets shall soon be yours to know."

As I touched her face she shattered into a million droplets of water and was gone.

The waters rose as though possessed. Voices and spirits swirled around me, "Donnachaidh Mhor, Donnachaidh Mhor, you must come," they hissed, "thou shalt find passage from your mortal world to the Otherworld, the water spirit shall be your guide."

The Kelpie rose up from the black waters as a horse once more and beckoned me to take her bridle. Slowly I mounted the mythical beast. Suddenly the reins writhed like so many snakes and bound my wrists tight. I could not move, "What is this?" I screamed, "Curse you! Curse you for your treachery Demon!"

She plunged deep into the faerie pools, down and down into the black water and into the cold darkness. This was to become my destiny, my curse. I became the Chosen One, Donnachaidh Mhor, the Jacobite Officer.

The Drowning
(Dream of the Waterhorse)

She called to me, guided me to where she lay,
within the magical waters of the faerie pools.
She took me to places I had never seen,
times in the future, times in the past,
mystic circles you have no understanding of,
ruined castles, murder, treachery, battles fought in ancient times.
I saw men long since dead, men yet to be born.
I am cursed to wander through time, never to touch nor feel,
I am but a shadow, lost in time itself.
Am I the bird that sings?
Am I the wind that blows?
Am I the storm?
I am all of them and yet I am nothing.
Close your eyes, come, walk with me,
through the mists of time,
you will see what I see, hear what I hear.
Like me you will become but a moment,
a moment from the dream,
the dream of the water horse.

The Lark

I am undone, possessed, for she is my every thought.
She guided me through the Otherworld,
where time has no end and no beginning.
I hold her bridle, through the mists of time I fly.
Am I the bird that sings?
Am I the wind that blows?
Am I the storm?
I am all of them, I am everything,
for I am the lark at the dawn of day,
the flickering candle to which you pray,
a ship at sea, lost forever,
the snow that falls lightly upon the heather.
Like morning sun and frosted shadow,
both cannot stay until the morrow.
Deeper and deeper I go into the blackwater,
serpents and beasts grasp at her halter.
I cannot breathe and I cannot scream,
I clasp the mane in this Kelpie's dream.
Take my hand, come with me,
through the darkness,
through the dream of the water horse.

The Crossing
(Ferry for the Dead)

I OPENED MY EYES.

I was not drowned but was still bound to the Kelpie. We stood at the edge of a swirling abyss; I could see nothing. Slowly a shape came towards us out of the mist, a cloaked figure on a boat. His bony hands clutched a great oar that moved him closer and closer. He looked to me but there were no eyes, no face. He was death, Manannán mac Lir, the ferry man to the Otherworld.

"We must go with him, Donnachaidh Mhor," spoke the Kelpie.

We stepped onto his ferry, and a thousand voices of the dead called out to me. I trembled and whispered to myself that I should not be afraid. The cloaked demon turned towards me. He spoke.

"Donnachaidh Mhor, I speak for those who are dead. In the earnest seeking of truth, ye shall learn that those without words shall speak, that those without form are seen, those without presence are felt, knowledge lost be learned. Ye shall walk with the dead and live greater for it."

The voices and screams faded and only the sound of the oar on the water remained.

Gask
(The Clach an Airm)

WE CAME ASHORE AND ALL WAS DARKNESS. MY HEART beat in my chest but I was surely dead, "Where am I, Demon?" I asked.

"You have crossed to the Otherworld, where the fate of mortals is but a reflection of what must be. Come, Donnachaidh Mhor, there is much to see."

"I care nothing for your faerie world, Demon. What of my cause? My Prince? The letter to Sleat?"

"My name is Niamh, not Demon! You shall see what a demon truly is! Remember the words of Manannán mac Lir, you shall see and you shall learn, for true evil lies in the heart of mortals."

We strode from the water and the darkness into the grey mists of day, heading high into the hills. There were standing stones all around. I knew that place. It was Gask, a stone circle above Inverness. My binds disappeared and I climbed from my mount.

"These are ancient stones from the time of the Picts, the painted ones," said Niamh, "but this is not their time. I must take human form once more lest I am discovered," I watched as the water spirit shapeshifted once more into the beautiful young woman.

There was little shelter; the wind blew through my wet plaid and chilled my bones. The sky was dark, heavy, cold. It felt like winter though I knew it was not. I could hear noise nearby and felt drawn to it, the voices in my head called me. I was compelled towards it.

Through the mist I could see another ancient standing

stone, its purpose I knew not. I could hear voices, then saw men using the stone to sharpen their blades, "It is the Clach an Airm, the Stone of the Swords, and today is the 15th April 1746," said Niamh.

They were coming closer, all speaking in the Gaelic language of their ancestors, the language of my people. I beckoned and called to them but they looked through me and beyond. There was purpose in their gathering, I felt afraid for them. They were lining up to sharpen their basket-hilted swords, their dirks, and spikes for their targes. There was a grinding noise of metal scraping on stone. As I felt the wind bite into my bones a little deeper, something told me that, for many, it would not be enough.

"The Clach an Airm has been used for centuries to sharpen the blades of the men of Strathnairn. Never before has it been more important than now. Tomorrow these men will fight and die for Prince Charles Edward Stewart in a terrible battle with the strangers," said Niamh.

All around Clach an Airm there was colour. There were hundreds of men, all dressed in the tartan garb of their forebears, the colours of their plaids dyed from the plants of the Strath. There were men of standing there too, in finely embroidered waistcoats with lace shirts and silver buckled shoes, so all the world could see they were the finest in Gael-dom. These were no ordinary men, they were the flower of the Prince's Jacobite army.

There were many also there to whom the Lord had been less gracious, they wore the long plaid. Many were barefoot and had little more than the honour they carried in their hearts. They would rather be tending their animals and stay-ing at home with their families. But refusal to turn out for the Prince would result in their roof being burnt from over their heads and their cattle being driven off, all by the men there dressed in lace.

For all their differences, tomorrow they would unite to fight as Clan Chattan.

I could see Gillies MacBain with Alexander MacGillivary. I knew MacGillivary when we were young men, he was a fine man and a proud Jacobite.

"Both will lead Clan Chattan into battle tomorrow," said Niamh.

To see them together! They were giants of men, more than six and a half feet tall. I would not wish to be their enemy. A stunning young woman was fussing over Alexander; there was blue light all around them. I had no wish to know what would befall them but I knew I had little choice. It was for the Kelpie to decide what I would see.

There were all ages there, some old men, others were young, very young. Mere boys that should be at home with their mothers. A restlessness broke amongst the gathering. The men clustered behind their leaders and moved out towards east Inverness.

"These men will reinforce the Jacobite army tomorrow, men who have endured a seven month long campaign of warfare across England and Scotland. The red strangers will meet the men of Clan Chattan with great fear and trepidation," again spoke Niamh.

It was early afternoon and the Clach an Airm stood alone once more in the open landscape, never to thus be used again in anger. The sound of sharpening of steel on stone has long been only a memory there.

As I turned, an ice cold sleet drove into my face. I had no desire to follow those poor souls; the sick feeling in my stomach told me all I could wish to know. The mists returned, "Donnachaidh, we must go."

Once more I was consumed and flew into the blue light.

Clava Cairns

I WAS THROWN FROM HER SADDLE AND FELL FORWARD onto my hands and into the mud. It was dark; I glanced up to see great fires burning. There were hooded men chanting in a strange language, dancing around a wrapped body. As the flames flickered and lit up their faces, I saw they were painted blue, with strange symbols upon them.

Standing stones were all around me, some twelve feet tall and leading to great stone brochs in their centre. The brochs are long known as a place of eternal rest for the dead.

"This is Clava Cairns. We are still in the Strathnairn valley, only 3000 years before. This is a place of ceremony, built by the painted ones," said Niamh.

I turned to hear screaming as a young girl was dragged from a nearby cart. She was bound and held down before the hooded figures. By her hair she was made to kneel as a large blade was brought to her throat, she was but a child. I could not let it happen.

I drew my sword and rushed her attackers. My broadsword cleaved a cloak and sparks crackled from my blade as it bit deep into the stone behind the figure. I pulled my sword blade from the stone only to see that the young girl was dead and her murderer unharmed. I slashed at him again in anger, but again my blade found no host. It was then I realised finally that I was a ghost, or perhaps that they were ghosts. I could not harm them.

Niamh took my arm and gripped me tightly, pulling me away, "We must only watch, Donnachaidh Mhor."

The painted ones took their staffs and pushed them into

(26)

the young girl's blood. They then waited in turn to anoint the wrapped body with the blood. Their pagan prayers were not for my ears, so I turned west to see the first beams of light pouring down the valley. The air was pierced with a terrible noise as they blew their ungodly horns, long bronze trumpets with the faces of serpents, a noise surely from the depths of hell. I covered my ears against their pagan rant.

"The Carnyx, Donnachaidh Mhor, the war horn of the painted ones."

The early morning light streamed through the standing stones as if they were some kind of ancient guard, brightness skipping across the stones to fill the passageway of the cairn, quartz shining like fireflies. The painted people placed the body in the centre and began to lay stones on top of the passageway, one by one, till the last beams of light flickered and were extinguished.

Slowly the hooded figures began to drift away, still chanting in their strange tongue. As the flames of the fire died away I could hear snarling and howling. There were yellow eyes all around, and the beasts of the night moved in from the forest, rushing in to fight over the poor girl's remains.

I dried my tears from my cheek; I could watch no longer, "Niamh, please, take me from this ungodly place."

Rait Castle
(Feast of the Bull)

AGAIN CONSUMED BY THE BLUE LIGHT, WE RODE AND spun through time and space. Voices called out, spirits flashed before me.

Finally my eyes opened and I found myself in a large room in a castle. There was a roaring fire, arch windows, a magnificent dining table laid out for a feast. A hog's head of claret sat at the head of the table and a roasting pig on a spit was turned by the fire. In the corner of the room, a group of armed men in Highland dress whispered. I heard mention of a bull's head, that something was to be ready. I could sense the treachery afoot, but against whom at that stage I could not tell. The candle-light glinted on their blades as they passed them around and hid them deep within their plaids.

There was a loud bang on the great doors at the entrance-way; the bar was drawn and the large doors swung open. A dozen men were welcomed in by their hosts and encouraged to fill their bellies as Highland hospitality demanded. One by one they took their place at the huge table and the feast began, but the atmosphere was strained. As a bull's head was brought in on a fine silver plate, the Chief quickly pulled his blade and plunged it into the neck of his nearest rival, over and over, blood gushed from the man's neck as he was hacked to the floor. Screams of terror and agony rang out through the castle, metal clashed and screams of agony filled the air as blades were plunged into flesh. The guests were armed too; they had ripped their dirks from inside their shirts and made fair the murderous judgement. They were more than a match for their rivals.

The table was thrown in the air and the hall set ablaze. How could the guests have known? The Chief grabbed at a young girl, his daughter, but she freed herself from him and ran to a bedchamber where she bolted the door.

The Chief bellowed, "Betrayal! Judas!" and smashed open the door. The room was in flames as she cowered in the window, threatening to jump. Her father drew his sword and took a swing at her; she jumped back, hanging to the window ledge. The next swing took off both her hands and she fell, screaming, to her death.

He turned towards me clenching his bloodied blade. I felt a sickened madding from within me, "Thou shalt live no longer! Murderer!" I screamed. I drew my dirk and plunged it deep within his belly, only for him to walk straight through me.

I stepped from the blue light into the empty smouldering shell of the hall with the Gothic arch windows. I realised I knew where I was, a place of real evil ... it was the cursed Rait castle and I had witnessed that legend, "the Feast of the Bull". The occasion had been meant to heal the troubles between the Comyns and the Mackintoshes. Instead the Comyns plotted to murder their guests. The Comyns' Chief's daughter was in love with a Mackintosh and had betrayed the plot to kill them to her lover at the whispering stone. Rait will remain empty for all time, cursed to rot like the soul of the Comyn Laird. His poor daughter wanders there still, forever looking for her lost love.

Gille Dubh

THE LANDSCAPE CHANGED ONCE MORE, FINALLY TO something familiar: Loch a Druing.

"Climb from me and be still, I must return to water lest I become like you forever."

I stare hard at the creature, "Who are you?"

"I am Niamh of the Golden Hair," she replied, "daughter of Manannán mac Lir, the Ferryman. Do not wander, for you are not safe here. There are beasts who watch us and would harm you. Wear this necklace and take my cloak, Féth fíada, 'tis my father's gift to me and will shield you from the eyes that would harm you. Build a fire and wear it."

Shaking, cold numbing my senses, I had to warm myself. I collected wood from the shore to build a fire and pulled the cloak around my shoulders. The fire crackled and the light danced and sparkled around me, passing through my very being. I was invisible. I knew not what I had become. Was this a dream, perhaps a dream within a dream?

I woke and pushed the cloak from me, looking beyond the shore to a mist-covered birch wood. It seemed to move before my eyes and a shape emerged from the darkness, a white stag, which stared at me from afar and snorted, its breath hanging in the air. I had never seen such a creature with its red eyes and cloven feet stamping the ground.

Suddenly a child's scream rang out. I looked to where the noise had come from then turned back to the stag. It had gone. I ran towards the wood but Niamh blocked my path.

"We must not enter human, this is the lair of the Gille Dubh."

The Jacobite Officer

"I say we must, for I heard the screams of a child," said I.

"The Gille Dubh will not harm a child, but it will kill you."

"I am not afraid of any creature. Perhaps I am dead anyway," I answered as I drew my sword and made towards the dark trees. The woods hissed and creaked before me. Niamh gave a final warning.

"If you must enter, beware of the Gille Dubh, for he is the very forest. He wears clothes of moss and lichen, black hair, and has piercing green eyes."

I walked silently into the forest as the light faded leaving Niamh, my curse and my protector, behind me. The wind howled through the trees and I cut my way through the vines with my sword. The branches moved as if alive; suddenly a vine pulled on my neck and yanked me to the bow of a tree … like snakes the branches closed around me, wrapping me tighter and tighter. I swung and hacked with my sword but to no avail, I was bound. I could not fight the tree demon. It pulled tighter round my neck, lifting me up, choking me…

Then I fall.

Dazed, I looked up, semi-conscious. A child was there, holding the hand of a small dwarf-like creature. He hooked my neck with the blade on his staff and his green eyes gleamed in the darkness, "You wear a moonstone necklace of the Otherworld, human. Where did you get thissss," he hissed.

Niamh answered from the shadows, "Tis mine, he saved my life and now I am bound to him. Let him go."

"Ye shame your own kind, ye should have drowned him."

"If you harm him, I shall drown you should you ever leave these woods."

"I never shall Kelpie, for this is my world, not yours. I advise you to be humble," at that the vines snaked through Niamh's bridle and pulled tight, trapping her too. But the child tugged on his arm and he removed his blade from my throat.

(32)

"Let them go, Gille Dubh," she asked. "I was lost and you found me, you gave me food and shelter, but they can take me to the edge of the woods and beyond to my home."

"As you wish, child," the vines released me and I rose to my feet, still much dazed from their noose-like grip. "Go with them child", he continued, before turning to me once more, "Be warned, son of man, never return, else you will become like those who came before you," he pointed with his staff at the vines writhing through shattered skulls on the forest floor. A solitary tear then ran down his cheeks as he embraced the girl, "Go, go child, and tell no one of the Gille Dubh."

I saw again the white stag at a distance, his red eyes watching us as he moved silently through the wood. The Gille Dubh gasped at the sight of him and scuttled away into the darkness. I looked again, but the beast was gone once more.

I take the child's hand and we walked towards the light, "What is your name child?"

"My name is Jessie MacRae, my father is Duncan Macrae of Eilean Donan, the slayer of Donald Gorm."

The blood ran cold in my veins. I knew of who she spoke, "Niamh, how could this be?" I asked. "This man lived two hundred years before I was born. It is some kind of madness."

"You must return her human, you chose to involve us. This is not your time and you are here to observe, not change. Mortals in the future will hunt the Gille Dubh for your meddling."

Eilean Donan

THE CHILD AND I MOUNTED THE KELPIE. WE RODE together through the misty night and on through Kintail until we came upon the great bridge of Eilean Donan. I took the child's hand and beat the great door with my basket sword.

"I must go child, you will be safe now."

Jessie hugged me tightly, "Thank you, Donnachaidh Mhor."

On turning to go I was blinded by a rainbow of light. I saw the bridge in flames, the headless ghosts of men wailing and weeping and beckoning to me for help. The bridge was covered with the severed heads of perhaps fifty men. Balls of fire rained down upon us from ships at sea ... What was this? Five hundred years of history in one night?

"We are time and time is us, you have interfered with that which cannot be undone," the voices screeched.

"Take me from this madness!" I seized Niamh's bridle and rode through the flames, she dived into the water once more ... down and down into the black water, spiralling, again, through time and tide.

Struan

"WHAT BECAME OF MY FATHER, NIAMH? HE IS AN OLD man. Does he know I am gone?"

"The Poet Chief is a man of great loyalty and courage, gifted in arts and poetry. You are he and he is you, Donnachaidh Mhor. Come. Look."

Through the mist and blue light I saw the Prince flanked by Cameron of Lochiel and MacDonald of Keppoch as they entered my ancestral home at Struan. I watch as the Prince entered my father's study. His private guard stood in the shadows.

Struan of Robertson sat by a roaring fire. The light flickered on his old face and bent nose, and he rubbed the clan stone, the Clach na Bratach, between his palms. He looked up as the doors were opened.

Lochiel spoke first, "Your Highness, may I present Struan of Robertson. There is no more loyal subject in Your Highness' kingdoms than he. The Poet Chief and Clan Donnachaidh have served your cause like no other. He has the distinction of being 'out' in the risings of 1689 and 1715. He is ready to serve once more."

My father rose to his feet with stiff old legs, only to kneel again at the Prince's feet with tears in his eyes, "Your Highness, I devoted my youth to the service of your grandfather and my prime to that of your father. I now pledge my old age to the cause of Your Royal Highness. I am your humble servant."

The Prince, quite overcome, embraced the old man, "I met your son Donnachaidh Mhor at Glenfinnan and commissioned him an officer," said the Prince. "He was dispatched

(35)

The Jacobite Officer

with a letter for MacDonald of Sleat but I fear some mischief may have befallen him. He has not returned and his horse was found near the faerie pools."

My father's face looked as though he had seen a ghost.

"What is it? I thought perhaps your son's horse had thrown him, he was young and spirited," said the Prince.

"As a child Donnachaidh Mhor told me of a reflection that he had seen, a horse spirit, at the faerie pools. He would have drowned had I not pulled him from the water. Since that day I have been cursed by the dream that one day he would disappear, taken by the spirits to the Otherworld, never to return," he slumped back into his chair, tears rolling down his face. "Please Lord, watch over my son and protect him from such demons!"

Keppoch laughed, "Otherworld indeed! Perhaps you had too much wine old man. I fancy he had no stomach for our cause and lies with a wench somewhere."

The Struan blader and a henchman stepped quickly from the shadows and pressed their dirks tightly against the throat of Keppoch and his gillie, "Remember where you are sir, Donnachaidh Mhor is the Chief's son. With a flick of my wrist I will open your throat and make the floor as red as the army you seek. Struan is a man of manners and principle. I care not if you are the Lord of the Isles himself, you will show respect."

The Prince put his hand between the blade and the neck of Keppoch, "Please gentlemen, put aside such bravado. We are here for the same cause and in the home of the greatest Jacobite Chief of them all. Keppoch jests; he will apologise."

With a grimace Keppoch bowed his head and sought pardon from the old Chief. The Prince then kneeled at my father's feet and took his hand, "Struan, will you rise with your Atholl men and follow me?"

"I shall, and so will every man whom I can raise," said Struan.

(36)

The Prince jumped to his feet, "Excellent, I feel divine providence is on our side gentlemen. God willing I will make you a free and happy people."

After they left the old Chief sank into his chair. He swirled a large glass of claret and fingered the Clach na Bratach as it twinkled against the firelight, "Oh Donnachaidh Mhor, where hast thou gone? Are you taken to the Otherworld, the land of Cú Chulainn and the forever young?"

In tears I screamed out, "I am here father!" and I rushed over to the old man, but Niamh grabbed my arm.

"He cannot hear or see you, Donnachaidh Mhor." But suddenly my reflection, through swirling waters, appeared in the Clach na Bratach. Father gasped and dropped the stone, "My son, I saw you there!" he picked up the stone but the vision had gone. In its place was a huge cracked flaw.

"My son, my Prince! The cause! Its a bad omen… the Clach has spoken, but I gave my word and I must rise up."

The mists returned, "We must go now," said Niamh.

"How could he see me through the stone?"

"The stone is a gateway to the Otherworld and to what must be. I should not have allowed you so close to his Oracle."

"I remember that reflection, the swirling water."

"Your father spoke the truth, for the reflection in the water was mine from long ago, but you were taken from me. We must go now. I will show you. Come. Take my bridle."

Cú Chulainn's Dream

THE MISTS CLEARED TO ANOTHER PLACE I RECOGNISED, the faerie pools. I stood at the water's edge with Niamh as I watched a child playing by the pools. He threw sticks into the water for his dog as a man and woman sipped wine and laughed from under a nearby tree.

The boy suddenly dropped the stick as though in a dream. He waded out into the water towards the waterfall, hand outstretched. I could see colours and dancing lights in the water, a dark shadow, eyes sparkling in the waterfall. The boy vanished beneath. There was no scream, no warning. It took a moment for his parents to notice he was gone, but when they did the man ran to the water, screaming, diving under again and again. The woman was hysterical, she was in the water too. After what seemed an age the man surfaced with the blue and lifeless boy. The colours in the water were gone. On the bank he thumped the boy on the back, again and again, until the boy heaved a huge breath and vomited water.

"I remember, the boy was me. This was my mother and father. I was five years old."

"It was not your time, but it was your destiny," said Niamh.

I was consumed with rage, "I curse you and your faerie kingdom! You are but a demon who would drown a child. You are the evil of which you speak!"

"You do not understand Donnachaidh Mhor, for your coming was foretold long ago in Cú Chulainn's dream. Your father, blessed by the sight, could see it all. You are the chosen one, I was chosen to guide you."

"You mean trap me and take me from all that I hold dear?

Show me my father, my Prince. What happens? I demand you show me!"

"If I must, but remember that knowledge and truth is a burden," cautioned Niamh.

Prestonpans

THROUGH THE MISTS THE JACOBITE ARMY TOOK SHAPE before me. They knelt to bless themselves in the morning harr. They had been guided to that spot and had outflanked the redcoats. They rose and in fury rushed forward screaming, hurling themselves towards the red shapes in the mist. Gaelic war cries and the blood-curdling skirl of the pipes rang out.

Cope's army, in panic, wheeled round to face the Highlanders, but they could only fire their cannons and muskets once before the enemy were upon them. Cope, screaming at his officers, pulled his pistol and demanded they make a stand. But it was chaos in the ranks. Terrified of the whirling mass of steel in the air they turned and fled towards the walls of Preston House, which blocked their retreat. The mass of silver blades become crimson with the blood of the slain.

A brave officer, Colonel Gardiner, fought on bravely, surrounded. He was finally felled with a scything blow from a Lochaber axe. All around me men were hacked to pieces until the Chiefs told their men to offer quarter.

Hands, arms, heads and legs lay everywhere. The young Prince despatched his surgeons to tend to the wounded. He shouted to all that those men were his subjects too and must be well treated.

Hundreds of red coated troops were dead, many more wounded, and around 1500 taken prisoner. The Highlanders suffered casualties of less than one hundred.

Father, content with the outcome, wrapped himself in Cope's bearskins in his personal carriage. He snorted Cope's snuff, sneezing and laughing at his good fortune. He was too

The Jacobite Officer

old to go on and asked leave of the Prince. I watched as the Prince embraced my father and bid him farewell.

A party of Atholl men take Father as far as they can in General Cope's carriage, carrying on until the roads are no more. They then pulled the wheels off and carried the carriage over the rough moor to home.

The Prince and the triumphant Jacobite army clattered up Edinburgh's Royal Mile as young lassies threw cockades at their feet. I should have been there. I cursed my misfortune.

Oisín

"SO NIAMH, I AM TO BECOME YOUR OISÍN? TAKEN BY A demon to live forever in your world of the dead, Tír na nÓg... I will tell you what I think of your world, 'tis no more real than the demons who inhabit it. Drowned in eternal half-truths and light, illuminated by a decrepit sun, it is a world of eternal mist and darkness and it is a nightmare from which I must awake."

"Donnachaidh Mhor, I am no demon! What I have done is borne of love. Oisín was taken from me by his wish to return to the mortal world once more. I lost him once and you are he, the son of Fionn mac Cumhaill reborn! He watches you in the form of a white stag. You have great power, you are everything, but envy is the curse of all things. There are spirits here to whom your coming is the eve of their destruction. You are hunted, they watch you. I must protect you but most of all I must protect you from yourself. You do not believe nor understand who you are. The Cù Sìth and other demons like them will follow you and wait for their moment."

"I am afraid of nothing, and I will split in two any who would come near me."

"You should fear them for you cannot kill that which does not live," cautioned Niamh. "I shall take you to Barevan to help you understand your mortal passage."

At that the mists descended and we flew through the heavens once more.

The Narrow Glen

In this still place, remote from men,
Sleeps Ossian, in the Narrow Glen;
In this still place, where murmurs on
But one meek streamlet, only one:
He sang of battles, and the breath
Of stormy war, and violent death;
And should, methinks, when all was past,
Have rightfully been laid at last
Where rocks were rudely heaped, and rent
As by a spirit turbulent;
Where sights were rough and sounds were wild,
and everything unreconciled;
In some complaining, dim retreat,
For fear and melancholy meet;
But this is calm; there cannot be
A more entire tranquillity.

Does then the Bard sleep here indeed?
Or is it but a groundless creed?
What matters it? – I blame them not
Whose fancy in this lonely spot
Was moved; and in such way expressed
Their notion of its perfect rest.
A convent, even a hermit's cell,
Would break the silence of this Dell:
It is not quiet, it is not ease;
But something deeper far than these:
The separation that is here
Is of the grave; and of austere
Yet happy feelings of the dead;
And therefore was it rightly said
That Ossian, last of all his race!
Lies buried in this lonely place

— *William Wordsworth, 1770–1850*

Barevan and Cù Sìth

I PASSED THE CURSED RUINS OF RAIT CASTLE AS THE first snows of winter swirled around me. I put my hand out to catch a snowflake, but it passed through my hand. Although I see and feel I do not exist as I once did. I yearned to be home with my wife and children, but feared I was lost forever.

It was bitterly cold and the snow quickly covered the passes and hills. I followed the old road above Cawdor towards Barevan. The bells of Barevan church rang out, but it surely could not be – Barevan had been a ruin for nigh on 300 years.

There were fresh tracks in the snow, as if made by a dog but huge, like a bear's. I followed their unfaltering path to the outer wall of Barevan. Could they have been made by the one that hunted me, that Cù Sìth, the faerie dog, that Niamh had warned me about? I had no wish to see such a demon...

But it was too late. I could hear the throated growl of a dog and a screeching wail as though from the depth of hell. It echoed and shook the old church walls ... I covered my ears ...'Twas the Carnyx once more!

I passed through Barevan's great walls and was met by a horrendous sight: a flaming gateway in the wall, an abyss ringed by demons, like flies on a corpse they swarmed and crawled. The stench of death was all around. Hurtling out of the abyss, snarling and spitting its frothed venom, came the devil hound Cù Sìth. It was no beast of this world. The Cù Sìth is a harbinger of death; it appears to take souls to the afterlife. He stood right before me, its flaming green eyes burning deep into me.

In one leap it came upon me, knocking me backwards,

pinning me to the wall. The stench of death from its breath was overpowering... It stared into my eyes as froth dripped from its fangs onto my face. I felt my very soul being ripped from within me...

My fist gripped my blade and I muttered the Lord's Prayer, "We are on holy ground, spirit protect me from this banshee..."

Suddenly Niamh appeared, rearing up and screaming at the Cù Sìth in a tongue from another world, a world to which I do not belong. She turned and kicked out her hind legs, knocking the foul hound back into the swarm of demons. It looked to the heavens before letting out a terrifying howl. Then it backed away from us, shaking its monstrous head as if in pain, and in one leap it jumped into the flaming abyss, howling three times and giving us one final stare of those burning eyes before disappearing.

The demons followed and the abyss vanished.

I fell to my knees, head spinning. The rancid stench of the Cù Sìth was overpowering. I was violently sick there, surrounded by the stench of death. Shaking, I forced myself to my feet. I was surely a stranger in a kingdom of demons.

Niamh spoke then, "Barevan is a magical place. The Thains of Cawdor are buried here. Once children would play here too. They would dare each other to lie in the punishment coffin. That was reserved for wrongdoers, who would be left overnight in the coffin. A huge stone slab would be laid over them with only their eyes showing. They would be left there for a day and a night with only the dead for company, to show them the error of their ways."

I lay down in the coffin, it was a fine fit but I was not ready for it, not yet.

"There is one here from your time who can open the door to the secrets that would have been your destiny."

I heard a name in my head: Elizabeth... Elizabeth...

I stood up and saw the church was a ruin once more, and I walked… to the old alter bowl. A beautiful young lady stood there. She looked at me but her eyes were red from tears. She was alone in some long-forgotten misery. She turned and walked to a gravestone which faced upwards, then lay down as if to sleep.

She was gone.

I read the name on the stone:

IN MEMORY OF

LADY ELIZABETH CAMPBELL OF CLUNAS

DIED 24 AUGUST 1746 AGE 24

I knew this woman, she was the lady I saw with Alexander MacGillivary at the Clach an Airm. What had happened?

"We must leave this place Donnachaidh, we must move quickly. I fear the Cù Sìth has your scent and I cannot stop him for long. He will not rest till he has torn your soul from you. He will return soon to tear the soul from Elizabeth."

"Am I alive or am I dead Niamh? You must tell me! What is to become of me?"

"You must speak with the Brahn Seer, I am forbidden to tell you. But I must show you your fate as a mortal."

The blue light returned once more and filled my heart with dread.

The Prophesy of the Brahn Seer

[nb. these words were recorded seventy years before the battle of Culloden]

O Drumossie,
thy bleak Moor
ere many generations have passed away,
be ye stained with the best blood of the Highlands.
Glad am I that I shall not see that day,
for it will be a fearful period,
heads will be lopped off by the score,
and no mercy will be shown or quarter given on either side

Culloden

AS THE MIST CLEARED I COULD HEAR GUNFIRE AND men screaming. I watched from the old Leanach dyke on Drumossie moor.

"Today is to be the blackest day in Scottish history. The 16th of April 1746, the Battle of Culloden. There are only 4500 cold and starving Highland men against 9500 well fed and rested Redcoats," Niamh announced.

I witnessed the slaughter as the men of Clan Chattan hurtled toward Barrell's regiment. The Redcoats' frontline stood three ranks deep and fired repeated volleys of grapeshot at the Highlanders, pieces of metal, chain, nails. The cannons shredded all in their path.

I felt sick. I heard the screams as men were torn apart.

Suddenly, out of the smoke, the Highlanders came. Like hungry wolves they ran screaming and the blood curdling Piobaireachd of the Camerons wafted over the moor, "Come ye dogs, ye dogs of the flesh, there is flesh to feed!"

The front rank of Redcoats bristled as the Highlanders hit them. The line was breached, Redcoats split crown to collarbone by broadswords. Arms were severed as they tried to keep the Highlanders back with their spontoons. The murderous cannons were silenced, their masters hacked to pieces.

Alexander MacGillivary came face-to-face with the commander of Barrell's regiment. He slashed his broadsword down hard upon the commander's spontoon and took the very fingers from his hand. Bayonets hacked at him as he broke the front line only to be surrounded and shot through the heart.

I saw him crawl away to die face down in a spring, the same

spring that one day would become known as "the well of the dead."

The Argyll militia tore down a wall to flank the Highlanders. Gillies MacBain stood alone in the breach and cut down all who flew at him, including Lord Robert Kerr. I counted twelve Redcoats that fell from his blade, one by one.

But another regiment, Cholmondley's, flanked the Highlanders and fired into their own men. They killed indiscriminately, friend or foe. The Highlanders who had broken through were surrounded. One by one they fell. Gillies MacBain stumbled with a vicious sabre cut to the forehead, he fell backwards against the wall, his leg broken. Despite cries from a mounted officer of, "Save that brave man," his attackers, enraged, bayoneted him repeatedly. He vomited blood until I saw the life leave his eyes.

Another MacBain lost his sword and fought bravely with the handle from a peat cart. I lost count of the men he bludgeoned until cavalry rode him down and trampled him.

Oh Gillies, thou shall be immortalised in these words:

With thy back to the wall and thy breast to the targe,
Full flashed thy claymore in the face of their charge:
The blood of their boldest that barren turf stain,
But, alas! Thine is reddest thee, Gillies MacBain!

All around was a scene of horror. The Highlanders fell back in disarray and the dragoons were cutting down all those who fell behind. The Chisholm standard bearer was cut down, his replacement too. The Prince was being led in tears from the battlefield to become a hunted fugitive. Behind him a thousand clansmen lay dead or dying, a quarter of their number.

The moor was covered in blood. The Redcoats look more like butchers than Christian soldiers and they splashed the blood at one another, the blood of the finest men in Gaeldom.

The Duke of Cumberland had issued orders that no quarter was to be given, callously written on the back of a playing card, the nine of diamonds, whilst he had been playing cards the night before. The horror was only just beginning.

Cumberland and General Hawley crossed the moor to view the writhing bloody mass of tartan. A wounded young man sat up, looking at the two mounted figures who approached him. It was the young Inverlochy.

"To which side do you belong?" bellowed Cumberland.

"To the Prince," came the reply.

Hawley turned to another officer, "Wolfe, kill that insolent dog."

"I am His Majesty the King's officer, not his executioner. You may have my commission before I will kill a man in cold blood."

"No need, for I shall do it myself," said Cumberland. He pulled one of his pistols and fired into the young man's head, spraying blood and gore over the young Wolfe, who vomited and retched till he had no more in his stomach.

Hawley laughed, "Such sport for a fine morning! You have much to learn young Wolfe. See that the Duke's orders of no quarter are obeyed. Any who dare ignore them shall hang."

Culloden House

"NIAMH, I CANNOT WATCH THIS, TAKE ME FROM HERE please," I begged.

"You must watch, for I told you that real evil lies in the heart of mortals. There is more to see."

Suddenly I was surrounded by Jacobites, some hideously wounded. I heard them say that they would be safe in the cellars of Culloden House, that the Laird there was a good man who would protect them.

We heard shouting and the doors opened. A redcoat officer and a party of infantry walked in with loaded muskets, "On your feet rebels, no need to be afraid. We will tend to the wounded, the surgeons are ready. There are carts waiting for you. Men that cannot walk will be carried."

For a moment I thought that perhaps a sense of humanity had returned. They were being taken to a large stone at the edge of the Culloden estate. A name came to my head...

The Officer Stone

ONE BY ONE THE MEN WERE HAULED OFF AND FORCED to stand against the stone. They were told to prepare themselves for death. They shook, wept, begged for mercy. There was none.

The redcoats laughed as they cocked their muskets, "Make ready!" commanded the officer and they aimed their muskets. I ran to stand between the men and the muskets, desperate to do something, but the musket balls passed through me. I felt nothing and turned to look behind me.

The men lay on the ground, some still moving, twitching, groaning, screaming.

"Do not waste your ammunition on these dogs, dispatch them as best you can with the butts of your gun, or bayonet them."

The savagery that followed made me look away. The prisoners were clubbed so hard that their brains were dashed out, or they were bayoneted where they lay. Their black work complete, the Redcoats left in search of more horror. Then I saw a man moving. It was MacIvor from the Master of Lovat's regiment. His face was hideously mangled but he was alive and crawling from the bodies.

A young man rode towards us and MacIvor screamed, "In the name of God end my life or carry me off!"

The young man's eyes were full of tears as he took MacIvor by the waist and gently lifted him onto his horse. I followed them for a short distance and saw the young man carry MacIvor into a corn kiln.

"Niamh, what will become of this man?"

I saw them through the mists, the man returned each day with food and water for the wounded MacIvor. I felt then that some good may come of it. Perhaps he would live. Then I came to see MacIvor as a cripple in his old age.

"He will go on tell the tale of butchery of the British Army," Niamh said.

Elizabeth Campbell

"PLEASE, NO MORE…" I CRIED, BUT NIAMH CARED LITTLE for my sorrow and the blue light surrounded me again. She walked me by the hand over Drumossie moor once more, where the stench of death was still strong.

A young woman was there, crying, sobbing uncontrollably. She cradled Alexander MacGillivary's head in her petticoat. It had been six weeks since the battle and Elizabeth had dug him from the pit with her bare hands. As she moved him he bled from his wounds as if they had happened moments before, the cold and the peat there had kept him as he was.

Lady Elizabeth was beyond help, her wails of despair terrible to hear. She blamed her vanity in wanting him to lead the clan. How proud she was and how cruel fate had become for them! Her family were forced to restrain and pull her away, she was screaming hysterically, inconsolably. They took MacGillivary's mortal remains and interred him under the step of Old Petty church, the ancestral burial ground of Clan Mackintosh.

Elizabeth would never recover, she was the vision of sadness I saw at Barevan where she lies.

Find peace Elizabeth, find peace.

On a stone ball in Barevan there is inscribed, "Jesus Christ, son of God, have mercy on me and all who lie here," have mercy indeed, on us all.

"This was to be your destiny Donnachaidh, death, had I not saved you. I could not let you die so cruelly," Niamh explained.

In the distance I heard the deathly howl of the Cù Sìth once more… it had much work to do that day.

The Brahn Seer

"you must speak to me of my destiny, niamh. the Seer who spoke of the future, perhaps he can tell? I know he was burned alive in a barrel of tar for his gifts to the world. Tell me, where lies he in the Otherworld?"

"There is but one who can tell you: the Skye witch Scáthach, who lies at Dun Sgathaich. She is all powerful and uses the spirits and beasts of the Otherworld to guard her domain, for she controls the gateway and therein lies the spirit of the Seer and the falls of truth. On one side lies your future; the other your past. Ask to summon the Seer."

"Take me there, Niamh."

"No, I cannot Donnachaidh Mhor. This is a journey for you and you alone. You must take my cloak, wear it at all times," at that a beautiful horse appeared before me, "and take this mount. Here too is Mac an Luin, 'tis the blade of Fionn mac Cumhaill himself. I will wait in the Faerie Glen for your return."

As I turned to head east a voice whispered to me on the wind...

The wind did howl and screech in pain
as the Skye witch Scáthach cursed your name,
'Twas your destiny Cú Chulainn's dream foretold
that a mortal must soon come to Otherworld.
Death and life are but the same,
a martyr's death… or servile chain.
A rotting corpse in tartan plaid,
wanders forth in darken shade,
a waterfall of glittering light
will speak of Donnachaidh Mhor.
Truth is but an everlasting lie,
locked in the darkness of Dun Sgathaich, Skye.

Dun Sgathaich

I RODE OFF THROUGH THE DARKNESS HEADING FOR THE coastal paths towards Dun Sgathaich. The skirl of pipes could be heard in the distance. The mist was thick and I could barely see… We moved slowly across the moors. My mount seemed nervous… suddenly she screamed and reared up at the sight of a red soldier with his head cleft in two, and another whose mouth gaped open, bloody from a sword cut… then there was another with no hands. They staggered forwards past us; the mist then cleared to show thousands of such spirits, 'twas the sea of the dead, moving towards Dun Sgathaich, drawn there by the pipes.

I heard their screams of agony, the ghosts passed over me like the very mist. I saw lassies in shrouds, stillborn bairns, plaided corpses hacked and foul. There was one I recognised as Keppoch, his face and hair matted with blood. I rode over to him, "Keppoch, 'tis me, Donnachaidh Mhor, what of our cause? Our Prince? Tell me!"

He wept and looked through me, "It is over," he muttered, "over," then he vanished into the sea of other lost souls. I thought we must be heading for the gates of hell itself, but still I followed those souls as they drifted towards Dun Sgathaich.

As we came closer I made out the form of a woman in black flowing robes standing on the battlements, 'twas her who played the pipes to the dead. They danced at the skirl of her tune, as if in some kind of spell. Lightning crackled off her pipes and all around the seas crashed against the rocks at Dun Sgathaich.

Suddenly the pipes stopped, "There is one here who does not belong," shouted Scáthach, and the spirits fell still.

"I seek only the waterfall of truth," I answered.

"You dare to speak in the presence of the dead?" Scáthach jumped from the battlements and the ghost sea parted as she moved closer.

"I carry the blade of Fionn mac Cumhaill, and I seek the Brahn Seer."

"Reveal yourself!" she hissed, "Who gave you that blade? It is for a far mightier hand than yours. I cannot see you, yet I know you are there… you wear another's cloak perhaps. Why do you seek the Seer? You cannot kill that which does not live!"

"I mean him no harm. I seek only my destiny witch, but the blade is for you should you desire it."

She laughed, "I think you are mistaken, for I do not fear death. I am death! Your cloak will not protect you from my hounds, they will seek you out, then I will watch as they rip you apart. Brahn, Scaolin," she commanded, "Seek out he who dares to speak to me in Dun Sgathaich."

She pulled on a great chain and out of the darkness two huge, green-eyed, stone beasts came to life. They howled, and the very ground shook with each of their steps. They circled me, sniffed the air, then snapped, tearing my cloak. I leapt from my mount and pulled the blade from its scabbard. That gave them pause, and they glared at my blade as if startled. I slashed out towards them. A surge of strength poured through me and I clove the great chain that bound them to the witch. There was a huge fountain of light and noise. The chain and the spell was broken, and their eyes changed from green to red.

They turned and snarled at the witch, then came to kneel by my side. Surely these were the great beasts of legend, the hounds of Fionn mac Cumhaill himself! They recognised their ancient master's sword. My arm was visible through the tear in the cloak, and the witch flew at me, aiming her blade at my head. I pulled Mac an Luin and a clash of steel rang out as my sword met hers. A crashing ball of light fragmented, then I slashed at her and caught her leg. She was thrown backwards and tumbled against the battlements.

That was when I realised – her leg was cut! If she could bleed, surely she could not be dead… but the witch quickly shape-shifted into the form of a hare and shot off in to the darkness. The spirits screamed and poured from Dun Sgath-aich like wasps from a byke. They surged towards me as they sought to follow Scáthach.

The hounds of Fionn mac Cumhaill rose to my aid, snarling as they kept the souls at bay. I mounted my horse and chased the witch, following a trail of blood through the mists and across the moors towards the Spar caves of Elgol. I caught a glimpse of her as she darted behind a rock and vanished.

Behind the rock a passage led down into a cave, and further down it opened into a huge cavern. There I found Scáthach, back to the wall, her leg still bleeding. I took off my cloak and she screeched, "So you are the mortal who walks with the dead!"

"And you are the Skye witch Scáthach, who trained Cú Chulainn," I answered.

"Yes, long ago Cú Chulainn prophesied your coming in a dream. I cursed your name as a child."

"I care little for your curses witch, I seek only the knowledge of the Seer. If you do not tell I shall make you bleed a little more."

"It is foolish to threaten a witch, for if I bleed then someone who loves you bleeds, Donnachaidh Mhor. I will tell you, but only as you wear Féth fíada, the cloak of Manannán mac Lir. If you move through this passage of caves, you will find the waterfall of truth. Speak what you desire to know. Perhaps the Seer will help you, but beware. Knowledge can be a cruel burden."

I left Scáthach and moved into a dark catacomb of dripping lime. Eventually I heard the waters then saw a blue light coming from a gurgling waterfall. There was a face in the water.

"Who are you?" I asked.

"I am he who you seek, burned in life for a gift I gave to those who desired knowledge. I am Coinneach Odhar, the Brahn Seer."

"I am Donnachaidh Mhor."

"I know who you are, you are Niamh's one, chosen to wander through time, to watch over those who cannot see."

"Where does this end Seer? I must return to those who need me."

"This does not end, you do not live. You are cursed like me, to watch, forever."

"But my heart beats, I live!"

The face laughed, "You do not live! You are drowned at the bottom of the faerie pools. The Kelpie drowned you, fool, to keep you forever."

I see the image of my rotten corpse in the water.

"You lie!" In a passionate rage I thrust my hand through the waterfall and grabbed the throat of the Seer... but the pain was unbearable and in horror I watched the flesh fall from my bone, and I stared at my skeletal hand.

"You are dead, Donnachaidh Mhor. You can only exist in the Otherworld. She has taken you to Tír na nÓg, the land of forever young. On one side you exist, on the other you are dead. Your mortal fate was far worse I can assure you. Your cause was destined to fail and the Highlands were to suffer for it."

"I must go back Seer, to my Prince, my clan."

"You cannot, your cause is finished and your home in ashes. The witch herself told you, someone who loves you bleeds," a vision of the Kelpie appeared then in the waterfall, she was lame and bled from a cut to her hind leg. "The Kelpie said she would give her immortal spirit to keep you safe and grant your wishes. She loves you Donnachaidh Mhor, but a love torn between two worlds cannot be, you must choose everlasting life or everlasting death."

I shuddered as the weight of his words fell upon me. He went on, "I have one last vision, Donnachaidh Mhor: the faerie dog. Beware of the Cù Sìth, he hunts you and he is close. Use the blade Niamh gave you, it is the blade of Fionn mac Cumhaill. She believes you are Oisín, her lost love, you have much to prove."

I left the cave and headed out into the starry night. After pulling on the cloak I rode north.

The land became boggy and I took off my cloak to guide my mount through to the moor. The stench of death was in the air, from what I knew not. Reaching drier ground, I again mounted up and rode north, following the stars.

Suddenly my steed was knocked from beneath me. She screamed and collapsed, and blood gushed from her neck as she was ripped apart. I staggered backwards... I had lost my cloak! Too late.

The Cù Sìth snarled and taunted me. He leapt into the air and knocked me to the ground, then snapped and tore at my neck, ripping my fingers from my hand.

Out of the mist a huge white stag appeared, through my fear I saw its snorting breath and red eyes. It hit the Cù Sìth with a power unimaginable, goring the evil creature and lifting it high in the air. The foul hound screamed in agony. It was my chance. I pulled Mac an Luin from my belt and plunged it into the breast of the beast, again and again... The beast lunged in its dying fury, sinking its teeth into my shoulder. Stinking blood gushed over me and the white stag as it writhed in agony. Souls of the dead poured from the beast's open wounds. We fell forwards, the Cù Sìth still gripping me in its dying fury. I lost my footing and we fell over the cliff of Kilt Rock down into the frothing water below.

The cold black waters of eternity had taken me at last.

I felt warm breath on my face and I opened my eyes to the huge white stag. He had saved me. I lay on the shore. I am dead but yet somehow I live. Had moments passed or a thousand years? There was no way for me to tell.

Niamh appeared then, "Fionn watches over you, Donnachaidh Mhor, for you are Oisín. You must accept it. You have freed yourself from the cursed faerie dog, now what more can I do to heal your mortal heart?"

"I desire only one thing Niamh, please grant me the power to punish the one responsible for the death of so many of my people."

"I will... close your eyes, take Mac an Luin tightly in your fist. Who do you see?"

"I see the Duke of Cumberland, he lies in his bed, bloated and stinking in his palace."

"Then thrust deep into his heart, his death will look natural for your blade will leave no mark."

I stood over him in his chamber. My knuckles were white with rage as I plunged Mac an Luin from one world to the next, stabbing his vile black heart. He gasped for air and I plunged again. He let out one agonising last scream and he was gone from his world.

I opened my eyes.

The sea of souls at Dun Sgathaich turned to see another arrive from the ferryman, 'twas Cumberland who staggered from the ferry in his nightgown. But a different path awaited him, and a black figure approached.

"Mercy, mercy!" he screamed, "'Tis the devil himself!"

The devil spoke, "No quarter given. You are a murderer of men, women and children."

The orders that Cumberland wrote on the nine of diamonds were thrown at the condemned man's feet, and he screamed in futile protest as the devil bid his demon servants to begin their black work. They plunged their red hot hooks into him and dragged him down into the burning cauldron to roast for an eternity.

"Come Donnachaidh Mhor, we must go," Niamh whispered.

"Let me ride Niamh, till the light comes. I must find myself."

"Please, do not go! I lost Oisín, I cannot lose you…" she paused then, resigned, went on, "If you must, please remember, you cannot touch the ground if you return. Promise me you will not."

I look to her sad face, "I must return Niamh, I cannot live forever without knowing what has become of my family. I must ride on to where I once lived to make sense of my life."

"Go if you must, but remember that much has changed and nothing can be done to relive the past."

Glen Dessary

I RODE THOUGH SPACE AND TIME, HEARING NOTHING but thundering hooves and my mount's breath.

Eventually I saw light skip on the water and I found myself riding along Loch Airceig. I went on to Glendessary, where once I lived. I felt happy and thought perhaps my wanderings were over.

I reached the river and looked towards my home, where A'Chuil stood. There was nothing, only grass covered stones. How many years had passed?

I could see the broken lintel of my old fireplace, and a vision came to my eyes, as plain as day. The Redcoats were burning my home. But where were my wife and my boys? I could not see them.

"Where are they!" I screamed into nothing, "Where are they? What have you done with them!?"

The vision faded and I heard my Jenny's soft voice distantly on the wind, and the children's laughter. It became louder and another vision came to me, of another home far away. I saw my boys play fight with another man in the gardens of a grand house. Jenny came out of the house with a young baby in her arms and put her arm around him, kissing him on the cheek.

Life had gone on in my absence; I was surely forgotten. The pain in my heart was unbearable.

Overcome with sadness and tears, I leapt from Niamh's horse and fell to my knees, forgetting her warning. As I touched the ground there was a rumble of thunder that shook around me. I heard the screams of a horse, a million voices at once, then nothing.

The Jacobite Officer

I heard Niamh's voice in my head, then she appeared before me, "I could not bear to live an eternity without you Donnachaidh Mhor. Destiny foretold you were to follow the path of Oisín. I gave my human form so that you might live, I made a faerie promise to Scáthach, who lifted your curse. It is I who must turn to nothing should you return to the land from whence you came. As soon as I took you from your mortal world, it was my destiny to become the wind, just as my father is the sea. Before you came I was destined to live between two worlds, trapped forever in the gateway of the faerie pools. You are my love, my reason for being, and my reason for dying."

"We were a love from two different worlds, a love that could never be," I answered. A solitary tear ran down her cheek and I reached out to touch her face once more, just as I had long ago. At my touch she shattered into a million raindrops once more… a swirling mist and was lost in the wind.

Stumbling to the shores of Loch nan Uamh, I fell to my knees, weeping, "O Lord, must I only understand love when it is lost? I have lost both in life and in the everafter."

Dream within a Dream

As I stand amid the roar of a surf-tormented shore,
grains of sand fall from my hand like moments in time.
The good, the gracious and the divine,
are locked together in a chasm of sleep,
and must awaken once more,
the slumbering hounds of Fionn mac Cumhaill,
Brahn and Scaeolin, and the blade of Mac an Luin,
the sleeping warriors and the horn of time.
The Brahn Seer gave us light through the darkness gleam,
though is all that we see but a dream within a dream?

Tech Duinn
(The House of Donn)

THE SKY DARKENED AND THE SEAS ROSE UP TO MEET the sky in a terrible storm. The ocean crashed around me. Out of the gushing, foaming waters, I watched as the black cloaked demon appeared once more, clutching his barnacle encrusted tiller. Above us, in the mist, a huge horse beat her wings. Niamh had become the storm itself, the very wind in his rotting sails. He had come for me…

The bony hand of the demon beckoned and the mist rolled in to claim me once more.

As I stepped onto the ferry for the dead, I understood 'twas my destiny to return, as my ancestors before me, to dwell in Tech Duinn.

I shall prepare for your coming. For all mortals must one day gather at the House of Donn in the Otherworld.

The mists are returning and I must go.
I stand in the forgotten glen of buried centuries.
I watch as plaided ghosts with bow and spear,
with shadowy hounds, hunt the shadowy deer.
I do not expect you will understand.
It will take time, generations, born and dying.
I can hear the Kelpie sing her strange song.
She sings to the beasts of her kind, she calls to me, I must go.
But I will see you again. When you close your eyes,
when you dream, when you take your last breath,
I shall be there, watching for all time,
For I am Donnachaidh Mhor
… and I am gone.

Author Background

AS LONG AS I CAN REMEMBER I HAVE BEEN FASCINATED by ruined castles and stories of beasts and ghosts. As a child I loved reading books and in particular poetry. My mum was quite worn out with her sons demands for never-ending bedtime stories. I loved to listen to tales told by firelight, sometimes ending up too scared to sleep!

Oral tradition and the written word by the great bards spoke to me deeply and I became intrigued by the many Celtic myths and tales that have passed into legend. I grew to love the work of Robert Louis Stevenson, Robert Burns, Lord Byron, William Wordsworth, Edgar Allan Poe, James Joyce and James MacPherson, to name but a few. I am quite sure the scholars amongst you will find their influence in my writing.

I have spent many a lost day wandering, from the inspiring old cobbled streets of Edinburgh to the lost wilderness of the Highlands. Scotland has a magical, unique quality that I will never tire of.

I was born in Dundee and lived in Carmyllie near Arbroath but moved to Dunfermline in Fife aged nine. Dunfermline was the ancient capital of Scotland, complete with a ruined 12th Century abbey, and is the resting place of Robert the Bruce, "King of Scots". Dunfermline was an inspiring "Auld Toon" to grow up in to say the least!

When I went to live briefly in the Isle of Skye in my late teens, I began to study the travels of the Bonnie Prince and the Jacobite risings. The cruel and bloody revenge of the British government struck deep into my psyche and I felt compelled to find out more and more.

Eventually in 1996 I become involved in a former Secret Jacobite Society, "A Circle of Gentlemen" of which I eventually became chair and I still am to this day.

In 1998 I met my wife Donna and in 2002 moved to my beloved Highlands to live. It was to prove to be a life changing decision. I had been a musician and a writer my whole life, with varying degrees of success, but a young family and a new business halted the creative path for many years. But I still had a secret ambition to create something unique in whatever shape that might take.

After completing an intensive four year course of professional study, my life felt full of spare time and possibilities, so in the summer of 2013 I decided to test my writing skills and attempted to write a book.

An entire summer later I had the bones of what would become *The Jacobite Officer*.

Fate was to intervene with a chance introduction to talented local composer Kenneth R MacLennan. We instantly clicked, and it led to the idea of creating a narrative soundtrack.

Some recording sessions then ensued at a studio on the banks of Loch Ness. There was a meeting of minds, chemistry and some magical moments happened.

As the recordings evolved, I realised that we were being taken in a deeper, darker direction, which influenced me to rewrite much of what I had already completed, so the whole body of work became very organic, one medium influencing the other.

As well as featuring the written word, the project evolved into a beautiful, moving soundscape, which became a successful live production in the Edinburgh Fringe Festival in 2016.

I have spent the last few years refining *The Jacobite Officer* and it has indeed been a journey into the darkest recesses of my imagination. You never truly know if its finished but sometimes you have to stop... there may be more to come, who knows? At the point of writing these closing lines, I have begun working on a supporting film project... *The Jacobite Officer* project continues to evolve!

I hope you enjoy the adventure; it truly was a labour of love.

Acknowledgements

The following people I wish to thank for their support and patience. I never would have got here if not for you:

Kenneth R MacLennan, Tom Alner, Craig Urquhart, Jason Dormer, Derek Joy, Andrew Stewart Jamieson, Ian Forsyth, Anthony Carson, Zoe Victoria, Alasdair MacNéill, Ross Shand, Paul Power, Victor Cameron, Deborah Dennison, Beverly Niland, Robert Jensen, Peter & Rae Gibson, Iona Gibson, Jack McDaniel, David McGovern, Paul MacDonald, Kenny Jamieson & A Circle of Gentlemen.

Also Kenny MacLeod, Tom Alner & Craig Urquhart for their wonderfully atmospheric imagery; Evelyn Spence for the 18th Century wardrobe; Norman C Milne for the 18th Century weaponry and accessories; Andrew Stewart Jamieson for his superb paintings of Charles Edward Stewart and Donnachaidh Mhor; Sandi Elliot & Susie Mackay, for the use of their stunning black horses Wardy & Troy.

Last but not least my wife Donna and family, who I am quite sure are all demented with my obsession with this man from the past.

I wish to dedicate The Jacobite Officer to the memory of my departed friends David Gilmour, Alex Mackay, Tommy Tweedie and Colin Rutherford who were a source of great support. They too walked into the light before their time.

Slàinte Gentlemen, my love to you all…

— *Matthew J Donnachie*

Praise for The Jacobite Officer:

Matthew's work evokes the tales which have transfixed the People of the Highlands for centuries. A dedicated Jacobite officer heads off on a critical mission only to encounter a different adventure altogether. With him we meet a beautiful, traitorous Kelpie and other creatures which have populated the stories the bards told in the glow of peat fires and passed down from generation to generation. Drawing on the history he knows and loves, Matthew has interlaced it with the legends of the mythology of the Gael like fine Celtic knotwork. Passion, adventure, great beauty and heartbreaking tragedy keep the audience transfixed in this compelling journey through time and his beloved Scottish Highlands.

– Deborah Dennison,
author and film maker.

Printed in Poland
by Amazon Fulfillment
Poland Sp. z o.o., Wrocław